Anonymous

Memorandum and Articles of Association of the English & Canadian Mining Company (Limited)

SALZWASSER
VERLAG

Anonymous

Memorandum and Articles of Association of the English & Canadian Mining Company (Limited)

Reprint of the original.

1st Edition 2023 | ISBN: 978-3-37514-626-9

Verlag (Publisher): Salzwasser Verlag GmbH, Zeilweg 44, 60439 Frankfurt, Deutschland
Vertretungsberechtigt (Authorized to represent): E. Roepke, Zeilweg 44, 60439 Frankfurt, Deutschland
Druck (Print): Books on Demand GmbH, In de Tarpen 42, 22848 Norderstedt, Deutschland

MEMORANDUM

AND

ARTICLES OF ASSOCIATION

OF

THE ENGLISH & CANADIAN

MINING COMPANY

(LIMITED),

AND

CERTIFICATE OF INCORPORATION

Under the Joint Stock Companies' Acts, 1856, 1857.

LONDON :

PRINTED BY E. COUCHMAN, 10, THROGMORTON STREET.

1858.

MEMORANDUM OF ASSOCIATION

OF

THE ENGLISH AND CANADIAN MINING COMPANY

(LIMITED),

WITH ARTICLES OF ASSOCIATION ANNEXED.

MEMORANDUM OF ASSOCIATION.

1st. THE name of the Company is " The English and Canadian Mining Company (Limited)."

2nd. The registered office of the Company is to be established in England.

3rd. The objects for which the Company are established are the acquiring and disposing of lands and mines and mining rights and privileges in Canada, and the discovering and working of mines in Canada, and the getting of ores, metals, minerals, fossils, and mineral and other substances, and the dressing, smelting, and otherwise preparing the same, and the exporting from Canada of the same, and the products of smelting, and the importing and preparing of all merchandise and other things requisite for and incidental to the operations of the Company and the dealing generally in mines, ores, metals, minerals, fossils, mineral substances, products, merchandise, and other things, and the facilitating of the settlement of lands of the Company, or near thereto, and the chartering of ships and other vessels for the purposes of the Company, and the doing of all other things, whether of such sort as are above expressed or otherwise, including the making and maintaining and disposing of buildings and works as the Company from time to time think incidental or conducive to any of the objects of the Company.

4th. The liability of the shareholders is limited.

5th. The nominal capital of the Company is £40,000 sterling, divided into 8,000 shares of £5 each.

We, the several persons whose names and addresses are subscribed, are desirous of being formed into a Company, in pursuance of this memorandum of association, and we respectively agree to take the number of £5 shares in the capital of the Company set opposite to our respective names.

Names and Addresses of Subscribers.	Number of Shares taken by each Subscriber.
ALEXANDER MORRISON . . . . 3, White Lion Court, Cornhill, London.	340
JOSEPH ROBERT MORRISON . . . . Theobalds, Herts.	240
JOHN LEACH BENNETT . . . . Merton, Surrey.	200
WILLIAM STOBART . . . . Cheshunt, Herts.	200
CHARLES TILT . . . . Fairlawn, Acton, Middlesex.	200

Names and Addresses of Subscribers.	Number of Shares taken by each Subscriber.
THOMAS LAURENCE .... 3, St. Mary Axe, London.	150
WILLIAM MORTIMORE .... 3, St. Mary Axe, London.	150
EDGAR PINCHBACK STRINGER............ 8, Austin Friars, London.	100

Dated the 25th day of June, 1858.

Witness to the above Signatures,

RICH^{D.} DAWES,

Angel Court, Throgmorton Street,

London, Solicitor.

ARTICLES OF ASSOCIATION

OF THE

ENGLISH AND CANADIAN MINING COMPANY

(LIMITED).

By an Act of the Canadian Legislature passed in the year 1855, the Quebec and Saint Francis Mining and Exploring Company, hereinafter called " The Canadian Company," were incorporated, and they are the owners of lands and mines and mining rights and privileges in Canada East.

The promoters of this Company have agreed with the Canadian Company to take all their lands and mines and mining and other rights, plant, and property, with a good title and free from incumbrances, upon the following terms :—The original capital of this Company is to be £ 40,000 sterling. The shares in one-half of this capital are to be issued to the shareholders of the Canadian Company as fully paid up shares. Out of the money raised by the shares in the other half of the capital, £ 4,000 is to be paid to the directors of the Canadian Company; the remaining £ 16,000 is to be the working capital of this Company. The terms and conditions of the arrangement are expressed in articles of agreement dated the 8th day of April, 1858, between the Canadian Company of the first part, and Alexander Morrison, Esquire, and others, of the second part.

Upon the above general principle, these Articles of Association are based, and all the shareholders take their shares on the full understanding that the above arrangements are to be carried into effect, and that those Articles of Agreement are accordingly to be binding on the Company.

INTERPRETATION.

In the interpretation of these presents the following words and expressions have the following meanings, unless excluded by the subject or context, to wit:—

" The Company " means " The English and Canadian Mining Company (Limited)."

" The Canadian Company " means " The Quebec and St. Francis Mining and Exploring Company."

" The Statute " means and includes the Joint Stock Companies' Acts of 1856 and 1857, and any and every other Act of Parliament, and Act of the Legislature of Canada respectively from time to time in force concerning Joint Stock Companies, and affecting the Company.

" These presents " means and includes the Memorandum of Association of the Company, and these Articles of Association and the regulations of the Company from time to time in force.

" Special-resolution " means a special resolution of the Company in accordance with Section 34 of the Joint Stock Companies' Act, 1856.

" Capital " means the capital from time to time of the Company.

" Shares " means the shares from time to time in the capital.

" Directors " means the directors from time to time of the Company, or, as the case may be, the directors assembled at a board.

" Auditors "
" Bankers " } mean those respective officers from
" Solicitors " time to time of the Company.
" Secretary "

" Officers " means the officers, from time to time, of the Company.

" Ordinary meeting " means an ordinary general meeting of the Company duly called and constituted, and any adjourned holding thereof.

" Extraordinary meeting " means an extraordinary general meeting of the Company, duly called and con- stituted, and any adjourned holding thereof.

" General meeting " means an ordinary meeting, or an extraordinary meeting, and any adjourned holding thereof respectively.

" Board " means a meeting of the directors, duly called and constituted.

" Local committee " means the local Committee of shareholders in Canada.

" Office " means the registered office, from time to time, of the Company.

" Seal " means the common seal, from time to time, of the Company.

" Month " means calendar month.

Words importing the singular number only, include the plural number.

Words importing the plural number only, include the singular number.

Words importing the masculine gender only, include the feminine gender.

CONSTITUTION.

The following shall, but subject to the provisions of these presents for the altering and repealing of the same, and to the exclusion of Table B of the Joint Stock Companies' Act, be the regulations of the Company.

BUSINESS.

ART. 1. The business of the Company shall be carried on by or under the management of the directors exclusively, with the aid of a local Committee in Canada, but subject to the control of general meetings in accordance with these presents.

2. No person, except the directors and persons thereunto expressly authorised by the resolution of a general meeting or of a board, and respectively acting within the limits of the authority conferred on them by these presents or by the resolution, shall have any authority to make, accept, or endorse any promissory note or bill of exchange on behalf of the Company, or to enter into any contract so as to impose thereby any liability on the Company, or otherwise to pledge the credit of the Company.

3. Where any person not so authorised and acting within such limits makes, accepts, or endorses any pro-

missory note or bill of exchange on behalf of the Company, or enters into any contract by which any liability might be imposed on the Company, a general meeting or the board may, as they think fit, at any time thereafter adopt or refuse to adopt his acts in that behalf.

4. The total amount at any one time of the liabilities of the Company on promissory notes and bills of exchange shall not, without the sanction of a general meeting, exceed £ 4,000.

5. All monies payable to the Company shall be received by the directors or by the local committee, or some person respectively authorised by the board, and shall be paid to the account of the Company with the bankers.

6. The receipts of two of the directors, or of the local committee, or person so authorised, or of the bankers, shall be effectual discharges for all monies therein expressed to be received, and from all liability, claims, and demands in respect thereof.

OFFICE.

7. The office shall be at No. 38, Broad Street Buildings, in London, or such other place as the directors from time to time appoint.

FIRST OFFICERS.

8. Alexander Morrison, of No. 3, White Lion Court, Cornhill, London, Esquire; Joseph Robert Morrison, of Theobalds, in the County of Herts, Esquire; John

Leach Bennett, of Merton, in the County of Surrey, Esquire; William Stobart, of Cheshunt, in the County of Herts, Esquire; and Charles Tilt, of Fairlawn, Acton, in the County of Middlesex, Esquire, shall be the first and present directors.

9. James Alexander, of No. 6, Great Winchester Street, London, Esquire, and Thomas Hall Gladstone, of Stockwell, in the County of Surrey, Esquire, shall be the first and present auditors.

10. Bank of London, in Threadneedle Street, in the City of London, shall be the first and present Bankers.

11. Messrs. Dawes and Sons, of Angel Court, Throgmorton Street, in the City of London, shall be the first and present Solicitors.

12. Joseph Robert Morrison, of Theobalds, in the County of Herts, Esquire, shall be the first and present Secretary.

CAPITAL.

13. The Company, from time to time, with the sanction of a special resolution, may increase the capital by new shares.

14. Any capital raised by new shares, except so far as the Company on the creation thereof otherwise determine, shall be considered as part of the original capital, and shall be subject to the same provisions in all respects, whether with reference to the payment of calls or the forfeiture of shares on non-payment of calls or otherwise, as if it had been part of the original capital.

15. The amount, from time to time, of the new capital shall, except so far as the Company on the creation thereof otherwise determine, be divided so as to allow such amount to be apportioned among the then existing shareholders.

16. The new shares shall, in the first instance, unless the Company on the creation thereof otherwise determine, be offered by the directors to the shareholders in proportion to the nominal value of their respective shares, and so many of the new shares as are not taken by the shareholders, shall be disposed of to other persons as the directors appoint.

17. But if the Company after having attached to any new shares any preference or guarantee or other special privilege, create any further new shares, the holders of the new shares to which the special privilege is attached shall not, unless the Company otherwise determine, be entitled to an offer of the further new shares.

18. A new share shall not be allotted to any shareholder at a discount, if any other person be willing to take it, at or above par.

19. With the authority of a special resolution, and the consent of the holders of any shares, the shares of such holders may be consolidated into a smaller number of shares, or divided into a larger number of shares, or be thereby or otherwise increased or reduced in nominal amount, or in aggregate nominal amount.

20. With the authority of a special resolution, and the consent of seven-eighths in number and value of the holders of all the shares, or, as the case may be, all

the shares of any class; all the shares, or, as the case may be, all the shares of the class may be consolidated into a smaller number of shares, or divided into a larger number of shares, or be thereby otherwise increased or reduced in nominal amount or in aggregate nominal amount.

BORROWING.

21. The Company shall not borrow on mortgage.

22. The Company, from time to time, with the sanction of a general meeting, may borrow on bond or debenture any sums they think fit.

23. The Company, from time to time, with the authority of the board, may re-borrow on bond or debenture, or on either of such securities, any sums theretofore borrowed on such securities, or either of them.

24. All monies borrowed shall be dealt with as capital money, and not as revenue.

25. The bonds and debentures to be granted by the Company, may be at such rate of interest, and on such terms and conditions as the Company determine, or failing such determination, as the directors think fit.

APPLICATION OF CAPITAL MONEY.

26. The amount of all calls on shares, and all monies borrowed, and all fines for leases, and all monies raised by sales of landed property shall be deemed capital money.

27. Except, as is otherwise provided by these presents, the capital money shall be applied by the directors as they think proper in paying to the directors of the Canadian Company the sum of £4,000 sterling, and defraying such of the expenses attending the formation and registration of the Company, and the preparation of these presents, and the obtaining of the transfer from the Canadian Company, and the obtaining of any Act of Parliament, or of the Canadian Legislature for any purposes of the Company, as in the judgment of the directors are properly chargeable against capital, and the paying off of money borrowed by the Company, or the providing for such paying off by making additions to the reserved fund of the Company.

28. The eventual surplus of the capital money shall be distributed among the shareholders in rateable proportion to the aggregate nominal amount of their respective shares.

RESERVED FUND.

29. Such a portion of the capital money and revenue of the Company, as the Board from time to time think fit, shall be set apart as a " Reserved Fund," to be applicable, at the discretion of the board, for the equalization of dividends, the meeting of contingencies, the making of explorations for minerals, or the extension of the operations of the Company.

30. Until the Company, by special resolution, otherwise determine, the amount set apart for the Reserved Fund, out of the revenue cf the Company, in any one year, shall not be more than one-tenth of the profits of the Company for that year.

31. Every advance out of the Reserved Fund to the account of revenue, made for the purpose of the equalization of dividends, shall be repaid to the Reserved Fund out of the first profits of the Company realized after the advance.

32. With the sanction of a special resolution, the board, from time to time, may apply for any purposes of the Company any part of the Reserved Fund theretofore contributed thereto out of revenue.

DEPRECIATION FUND.

33. Such a portion of the profits of the Company, as the board from time to time think fit, shall be set apart as a " Depreciation Fund," to be applicable, at the discretion of the board, for rebuilding or restoring any part of the works and plant of the Company, and for repairing the same and otherwise keeping it in good condition.

34. Until the Company by special resolution otherwise determine, the amount set apart for the Depreciation Fund out of the profits of the Company in any one year shall not be more than one-fifth of the profits of the Company for that year.

Investment of Money.

35. All capital money and all monies carried to the Reserved Fund and the Depreciation Fund respectively, and all other monies of the Company not immediately applicable for any payment to be made by the Company, shall be invested by the directors on such securities, real or personal, or on such mere personal security as the board from time to time think proper.

36. But no part of the monies of the Company shall at any time be advanced to any director, or to any person who within one year before the time of the advance was a director, or to any partner, clerk, or servant of any director, or of any such late director. Nevertheless, an advance to any Joint Stock Bank, or Joint Stock Company, of which any director or any such late director may be a shareholder, shall not be deemed an advance to himself and his respective partners.

37. The board may keep at the bankers such a balance as the board from time to time think fit, and notwithstanding any of the bankers may be directors, or a director.

38. The board may appoint and remove bankers in Canada as well as in London.

39. The board may allow the local Committee to keep at the bankers in Canada such a balance as the board think fit.

40. Capital money may be invested, as provided by these presents in the purchase of shares.

GENERAL MEETINGS.

41. The ordinary meeting shall be ǀ ' yearly in London, at such hour and on such day in every year, as the directors from time to time appoint.

42. But, until the Company otherwise appoint, the day for the ordinary meeting shall be the second Tuesday in January, or within one month after that day.

43. An extraordinary meeting may, at any time, be called by the directors of their own accord.

44. An extraordinary meeting shall be called by the directors whenever a requisition of any number of shareholders, holding in the aggregate not less than one-fifth of the shares, and stating fully the object of the meeting, and signed by the requisitionists, is delivered to the Secretary, or left at the office for the directors.

45. Whenever the directors neglect for fourteen days after the delivery of any such requisition to call a meeting, in accordance therewith, the requisitionists, or any shareholders holding in the aggregate not less than one-fifth of the shares may call the meeting.

46. Every general meeting shall be held at such convenient place in London, as the directors, or the requisitionists calling the meeting, appoint.

47. Three shareholders shall be a quorum for a general meeting, for the choice of a chairman for the meeting, and the declaration of a dividend.

48. Except for the choice of a chairman for the meeting, or the declaration of a dividend, the quorum for any general meeting, when the number of the share-

holders resident in the United Kingdom is less than 100, shall be five shareholders, and when the number of the shareholders resident in the United Kingdom is 100 or upwards, shall be twelve shareholders.

49. No business shall be transacted at any general meeting unless the quorum for the business be present at the commencement and close of the business.

50. If, within one hour after the time appointed for the holding of a general meeting, the quorum be not present, the meeting, if convened on the requisition of shareholders, shall be dissolved, and in any other case shall stand adjourned to the following day, at the same place, and to meet at the same time as was appointed for the holding of the original meeting.

51. If, at any adjourned general meeting, the quorum be not present within one hour after the time for holding the meeting, it shall stand adjourned *sine die*.

52. The chairman, with the consent of the meeting, may adjourn any general meeting, from time to time, and from place to place.

53. No business shall be transacted at any adjourned general meeting other than the business left unfinished at the general meeting from which the adjournment took place.

54. The directors calling any general meeting, and the shareholders calling any extraordinary meeting, shall respectively give at least seven days, and not more than fifteen days notice of the meeting.

55. Where, by these presents, notice of any business to be transacted at a general meeting is to be given, the notice shall fully particularize the business.

56. When any general meeting is adjourned for more than seven days, the directors shall give at least four days' notice of the adjourned meeting.

57. A notice, calling a general meeting, shall be exclusive of the day of giving the notice and the day of meeting respectively.

58. Notices calling general meetings shall be given by circulars to the shareholders resident in the United Kingdom, expressing the time and place of meeting. But the directors calling a general meeting, may also if they think fit give notice of the meeting by advertisement.

59. Any such circular may be sent by post, as a letter, addressed to the shareholder, according to his address in the register of shareholders, and if so sent shall be deemed to be delivered to him on the day on which in the regular course of the post office it would be delivered at his address.

POWERS OF GENERAL MEETINGS.

60. Any general meeting, when notice in that behalf is given, may remove any director or auditor for misconduct, negligence, incapacity, or other cause deemed by the meeting sufficient, and may supply any vacancy in the office of director or auditor, and may fix the remuneration of the directors and auditors respectively, and may vary the number of directors, and subject to the provisions of these presents, may generally decide on any affairs of or relating to the Company.

61. Any ordinary meeting, without any notice in that behalf, may elect directors and auditors, and may

receive, and either wholly or partially reject or adopt and confirm the accounts, balance sheets, and reports of the directors and auditors respectively, and may decide on any recommendation of the directors of or relating to any dividend, and subject to the provisions of these presents, may generally discuss any affairs of or relating to the Company.

62. When a general meeting, by special resolution, has determined on an increase of the capital, the meeting, or any other general meeting may, by special resolution, determine on the extent to which the increase shall be effected by the issue of new shares, and the conditions on which the capital shall be so increased, and the time, mode, and terms at, in, and on which the new shares shall be issued, and how the premium (if any) on the new shares shall be applied.

63. A general meeting, determining on the conditions on which any new shares shall be issued, may, by special resolution, determine that the new shares shall be issued as one class or as several classes, and may attach to the new shares, or to the new shares of all or any of the classes, any special privileges with reference to preferential, guaranteed, fixed, fluctuating, redeemable, or other dividend or interest or otherwise, or any special conditions or restrictions.

64. If after a general meeting has, by special resolution, determined on the issue of new shares, all the new shares are not issued accordingly, a general meeting by special resolution may determine that the unissued new shares shall not be issued, but shall be cancelled, or may determine on any alteration of the

conditions on which the unissued new shares shall be issued, or of the special privileges or restrictions attached to the unissued new shares.

65. Provided that no special resolution for the increase of the capital, nor any special resolution affecting any new shares shall be passed without the previous recommendation of the directors.

66. When a general meeting has by special resolution determined on borrowing any money, the meeting or any other general meeting may, by special resolution determine on the time, mode, terms, and rate of interest at, in, and on which it shall be borrowed; but no money shall be borrowed without the previous recommendation of the directors.

67. The Company may, in general meeting, from time to time, by special resolution, alter and make new provisions in lieu of or in addition to any regulations of the Company, whether contained in these Articles of Association or not.

68. The authority of a general meeting, from time to time, by special resolution, to alter and make new provisions in lieu of or in addition to any of the regulations of the Company, shall extend to authorize every alteration whatsoever of these presents, except only the regulations of the Company, which provide for the proportionate equality of the liabilities of the shareholders and of their interest in the profits of the Company, which shall accordingly be deemed the only fundamental and unalterable regulations of the Company; but the Company shall be bound by all their special resolutions, under which any shares were issued with

special privileges, and all new regulations of the Company shall have effect accordingly.

Procedure at General Meetings.

69. At every general meeting, the chairman of the directors, or during his absence a director elected by the shareholders present, or during the absence of all the directors, a shareholder present, elected by the shareholders present, shall take the chair.

70. At every general meeting, the director (if any) in the chair, although retiring from office at that meeting, shall remain in office until the close of the meeting, when, although the meeting be adjourned, he shall retire from office.

71. The first business at every general meeting after the chair thereat is taken, shall be the reading of the minutes of the then last general meeting, and, if the minutes do not appear to the meeting to have been signed according to the statute, shall, on being found or made correct, be signed by the chairman of the meeting at which they are read.

72. Except where otherwise provided by these presents, every question to be decided by any general meeting, unless resolved on without a dissentient, shall be decided by a simple majority of the shareholders personally present thereat, and, unless when a ballot is required, shall be so decided by a show of hands.

73. Every special resolution, and every question required by these presents to be decided by any other

than a simple majority of the shareholders personally present at a general meeting, shall be decided by ballot.

74. On every question to be decided by a simple majority of the shareholders personally present at any meeting, every shareholder personally present thereat shall be entitled to vote.

75. At any general meeting, unless a ballot on any resolution thereof be immediately, on the declaration by the chairman of the meeting of the result of the show of hands thereon demanded by at least two shareholders, and also before the close or adjournment of the meeting by a written requisition, signed by at least five shareholders, holding together shares to the aggregate nominal amount of £1,000, and delivered to the chairman, or to the secretary, a declaration by the chairman that a resolution is carried, and an entry to that effect in the minutes of the proceedings of the meeting shall be sufficient evidence of the fact so declared, without proof of the number or proportion of the votes given for or against the resolution.

76. If a ballot be duly demanded, it shall be taken in such manner, at such place, and immediately, or at such time within seven days thereafter, as the chairman of the meeting directs, and the result of the ballot shall be deemed the resolution of the general meeting at which the ballot was demanded.

Voting at General Meetings.

77. On every question to be decided by ballot, every shareholder present thereat in person, or by proxy, and

entitled to vote thereat, shall have one vote for every share held by him up to ten, and one vote in addition for every five shares above ten up to one hundred, and one vote in addition for every ten shares above one hundred.

78. If more persons than one are jointly entitled to a share, the person whose name stands first in the registe_ of shareholders as one of the holders of the share, and no other, shall be entitled to vote in respect thereof.

79. Whenever any parent, guardian, committee, husband, executor, or administrator, respectively, of any infant, lunatic, idiot, female, or deceased shareholder, desires to vote in respect of the share of such infant, lunatic, idiot, female, or deceased shareholder, he may become a shareholder in respect of the share, as provided by these presents, and may vote accordingly.

80. A shareholder personally present at any general meeting may decline to vote on any question thereat, but shall not by so declining be considered absent from the meeting.

81. A shareholder shall not vote in person, or by, or as a proxy at any general meeting, or ballot on any question in which he has any interest other than his interest in common with the other shareholders.

82. Whenever any question arises as to a shareholder being disqualified by interest from voting on any question, it may, on the request of any two shareholders, be referred to, and be decided by, the general meeting at which the question arises, or the then next general meeting.

83. A shareholder may from time to time appoint any other shareholder as his proxy in voting at any ballot.

84. Every instrument of proxy shall be in writing, according to the following form, and be signed by the shareholder appointing the proxy, and shall be deposited at the office at least forty-eight hours before the day for holding the general meeting whereat it is to be acted on, and shall be kept with the records of the Company, but shall be produced on every reasonable request, and at the expense (if any) of the shareholder, or of his proxy.

85. The following shall be the form of the instrument of proxy :—

" I (A. B.), a shareholder in the English and Canadian " Mining Company, Limited, hereby appoint (C. D.), " another shareholder in the Company, to act as my " proxy at the general meeting of the Company to be " holden on the   day of   , 18 , and " at every adjournment thereof [*or (as the case may be)* " at every general meeting of the Company]. As witness " my hand, this   day of   , in the year " of our Lord, 18   .

" (Signed)   (A. B.)"

86. Every such instrument of proxy shall be valid until it be revoked by writing under the hand of the appointing shareholder, deposited at the office, and to be kept with the records of the Company, but to be produced on every reasonable request, and at the expense (if any) of the shareholder or of his proxy.

87. The person in the chair at a general meeting

shall in every case of an equality of votes on a ballot, or otherwise, have an additional or casting vote.

MINUTES OF GENERAL MEETINGS.

88. Every entry in the minute books of the proceedings of general meetings, purporting to be entered and signed, according to the statute or these presents, shall, in the absence of proof to the contrary, be deemed to be a correct record, and an original proceeding of the Company accordingly, and in every case the burden of proof shall be wholly on the person making any objection to the entry.

DIRECTORS.

89. There shall be not less than three, nor more than five directors.

90. Every director shall be resident in England, and shall hold sixty shares in his own right, and as the sole holder thereof, to the aggregate nominal amount of £ 300 at least.

91. At the ordinary meeting, to be held in the year 1859, and at the ordinary meeting in every subsequent year, two of the directors shall retire from office, and the meeting shall elect to supply their places, an equal number of qualified shareholders.

92. The rotation for the retirement of the first and present directors, shall be determined among them-

selves, at a board held in the present year, 1858, by agreement, or failing agreement, by lot.

93. Every retiring director, if qualified, shall be eligible for re-election.

94. A shareholder, not being a retiring director, shall not be qualified to be elected a director, unless he give to the secretary, or leave at the office, not less than twenty-one days, nor more than two months before the day for election of directors, notice in writing, under his hand, of his willingness to be elected a director.

95. Whenever an ordinary meeting in any year fail to elect directors, in lieu of the retiring directors, the meeting shall stand adjourned to the next day, at the same place, and to the same hour, as were appointed for the holding of the meeting adjourned; and, if at the adjourned meeting, the proper number of directors be not chosen, the directors to retire shall continue in office until the first ordinary meeting in the following year.

96. Every director shall vacate his office upon ceasing to hold sixty shares in his own right, as the sole holder thereof, to the aggregate nominal amount of £ 300, or becoming bankrupt or insolvent, or suspending payment, or compounding with his creditors, or being declared lunatic.

97. A director may at any time give notice in writing of his wish to resign, by delivering it to the chairman of the directors, or to the secretary, or leaving it at the office; and on the acceptance of his resignation by the board, but not before, his office shall be vacant.

98. Any occasional vacancy in the office of director,

shall be filled up by the directors, by the appointment of a qualified shareholder, who shall, in all respects, stand in the place of his predecessor.

Boards and Committees.

99. Boards shall be held at the office when the directors think fit; but not less often than once in every two months.

100. An extraordinary board may at any time be called by any two directors, by two days' notice to the other directors.

101. The quorum of every board shall be three directors.

102. At the first board after every yearly election of directors, a chairman of the directors shall be elected for the year.

103. In every case of the absence from the board of the chairman, a temporary substitute for the chairman shall be appointed by the board.

104. The procedure of the board shall be regulated, so far as the standing orders of the board determine, by such standing orders, and in other respects as the directors present think fit.

105. Every question at board shall be determined by a majority of the votes of the directors present.

106. In case of an inequality of votes at a board, the acting chairman thereat shall have a second, or casting vote.

107. No director shall vote on any question in which he has an interest, adverse to the interest of the shareholders at large.

108. Minutes of the proceedings of every board, and of the attendance of the directors thereat respectively, shall thereat, or with all convenient speed thereafter, be recorded by the secretary, in a book kept for the purpose, and be signed by the chairman thereat, or in case of his default or incapacity, by any two directors present thereat, and be reported to the next general meeting.

109. Every such minute, when so recorded and signed, shall, in the absence of proof of error therein, be considered original proceedings.

110. Every board may adjourn at pleasure for such time, and to such place, as the directors present determine.

111. The directors may appoint and remove such committees of their own number as they think fit, and may determine and regulate their quorum duties and procedure.

Local Committee.

112. The directors may appoint and remove a local committee of shareholders, resident in Canada, for conducting all or any of the business of the Company there, and may delegate to the local committee such of the authorities of the board as the directors think requisite for the conduct of such local business, and

may determine and regulate their number, quorum, duties, and procedure.

113. But if, and whenever, the shareholders resident in Canada, or the majority in number and value of them, send to the board a list under their hands, of not less than six shareholders resident in Canada, as proposed for the local committee, the board shall choose the members of the local committee from the shareholders named in the list.

114. Every such appointment and removal, and every such delegation of authority, shall be in writing, under the hands of two at least of the directors, and countersigned by the secretary, and an entry thereof shall be made in the minutes of the proceedings of the directors.

115. The local committee shall have full power to act within the limits of the authority expressly delegated to them in writing, according to these presents, by the board; but shall have no power to impose any obligation or liability on the Company beyond those limits.

116. The local committee shall indemnify the Company against all obligations and liabilities, if any, imposed on the Company, by reason of the local committee transgressing those limits; and the members of the local committee shall be jointly and severally liable to effect such indemnification.

117. The local committee shall keep such minutes of their proceedings, and such accounts, and shall make such returns to the board as the directors from time to time appoint.

POWERS AND DUTIES OF DIRECTORS.

118. The directors shall be intrusted with, and exercise and perform the following powers and duties, (to wit :)—

I. The general conduct and management of the business of the Company.

II. The appointment, and removal, and the determination of the duties and salaries of the secretary, clerks, agents in Canada and elsewhere, and servants of the Company, and the securities to be taken from them respectively.

III. The appointment and removal of the solicitors.

IV. The calling of general meetings.

V. The instituting, conducting, defending, compromising, and abandoning of legal proceedings by and against the Company and the officers, and otherwise concerning the affairs of the Company.

VI. The purchasing, hiring, or building, as and when thought most advantageous, of offices for transacting the business of the Company, and the selling or otherwise disposing of the same.

VII. The purchasing, or renting, and holding of lands, mines, mining rights, tenements, and hereditaments, for the purposes of the Company, and the selling, letting, or otherwise disposing of the same.

VIII. The insuring against loss and damage by fire of the insurable property of the Company.

IX. The entering into contracts for the Company,
and the contracting on behalf of the Company of
such debts and liabilities as may be necessary
for transacting the business of the Company.

X. The making and giving of receipts, releases,
and other discharges for monies payable to the
Company, and for the claims and demands of
the Company.

XI. The compounding of any debt due to the
Company, and of any claims and demands of
the Company.

XII. The reference of any claims and demands of
and against the Company to arbitration, and
the performing and observing of the awards
thereon.

XIII. The acting on behalf of the Company in all
matters relating to bankrupts and insolvents.

XIV. The employing and investing of the paid-up
capital, and other monies received by the Company, in or upon such securities, authorised by
these presents, as the directors from time to
time approve.

XV. The appointing, removing, and regulating of
the local committee, according to these presents.

XVI. The keeping of proper accounts of the
receipts, credits, payments, liabilities, profits,
losses, property, effects, claims, and demands of
the Company.

XVII. The making up to the 31st day of Decem-
ber in every year of the accounts.

XVIII. The procuring of the accounts to be duly audited, according to these presents.

XIX. The making to every ordinary meeting of a full report of the affairs and prospects of the Company, including all such details as are sufficient to explain the accounts.

XX. The declaring and paying, when thought fit, of a dividend on account.

XXI. The making of calls on the shareholders.

XXII. The accepting of payments in advance of calls, and the determining of the terms on which such payments shall be accepted.

XXIII. The recommending, for the approval of general meetings, of matters to be determined by special resolution.

XXIV. The keeping of the register of shareholders, and of the register of transfers.

XXV. The authorising of the use of the seal; but so that every instrument to which the seal is affixed be signed by at least two of the directors, and countersigned by the secretary.

XXVI. The providing for the safe custody of the seal.

XXVII. The doing of all things requisite for compliance with the requirements of the statute.

XXVIII. The controlling, managing, and regulating in all other respects, except as by these presents otherwise provided, of all other matters relating to the Company, and the affairs thereof.

119. The directors shall, in addition to those powers and duties, exercise and perform all such other powers

and duties as, by the statute and these presents respectively, are directly or by implication conferred and imposed on directors.

120. The persons from time to time acting in good faith as directors, shall have the powers of directors, notwithstanding any defect in their appointment or qualification.

121. Every account of the directors, when audited and approved by a general meeting, shall be conclusive, except as regards any error discovered therein within two months next after such approval thereof.

122. Whenever any such error is discovered within that period, the account shall be forthwith corrected, and thenceforth shall be conclusive.

123. Any sum may be allowed by a general meeting to the directors for their remuneration, and with or without an additional payment to the chairman.

124. The remuneration for the directors, except the additional payment, if any, to the chairman, shall be divided between them, in such proportions as they from time to time determine.

125. Any sum may be allowed by a general meeting to the local committee, to be divided between themselves as they think fit.

AUDITORS.

126. Two auditors, not necessarily shareholders, shall be appointed by every ordinary meeting for the succeeding year.

127. Their salaries shall be paid by the meeting, but in no case shall be less than £10 a year for each auditor.

128. They shall audit the accounts of the Company according to these presents.

129. Any occasional vacancy in the office of auditor shall be supplied by an extraordinary meeting called for the purpose.

130. During any vacancy, the auditor in office shall exercise and perform the powers and duties of the auditors.

131. At least twenty-one days before the day for every ordinary meeting there shall be delivered by the directors to the auditors the half-yearly accounts and balance sheet, to be produced at the meeting, and the auditors shall receive and examine the same.

132. Within ten days after the receipt of the accounts and balance sheet, the auditors shall either confirm them, and report generally thereon, or, if they do not see proper to confirm them, shall report specially thereon, and shall deliver to the directors the accounts and balance sheet, with the auditors' report thereon.

133. Seven days before every ordinary meeting a printed copy of the accounts and balance sheet, audited, and the auditors' report thereon, shall be sent by the directors to every shareholder resident in the United Kingdom, according to his registered address.

134. At every ordinary meeting the auditors' report shall be read to the meeting, with the directors' report.

135. Throughout the year, and at all reasonable times of the day, the auditors shall have access to, and in-

spection of, the books of account and books of registry of the company, with such assistance by clerks and others, and such facilities as the auditors reasonably require.

OFFICERS.

136. The directors, auditors, members of the local committee, secretary, and other officers, shall be indemnified by the Company from all losses and expenses incurred by them in or about the discharge of their respective duties, except such as happen from their own respective wilful act or default.

137. No officer shall be liable for any other officer, or for joining in any receipt or other act for conformity, or for any loss or expense happening to the Company, unless the same happen from his own wilful act or default.

138. The accounts of any officer may (except as otherwise provided by these presents) be settled and allowed, or disallowed, either wholly or in part, by a board.

139. An officer becoming bankrupt or insolvent, or publicly compounding with his creditors, shall thereupon be disqualified from acting as, and shall cease to be, an officer.

140. Provided that, until an entry of the disqualification be made in the minutes of the directors, his acts in his office shall be as effectual as if he acted as a qualified officer.

141. The secretary shall keep the records, books, and papers of the Company, and shall allow, between the hours of ten in the forenoon and twelve at noon, such inspection of the register of shareholders, as is provided by the statute, so as every shareholder or other person, before inspecting it, sign his name in a book kept for the purpose.

142. The secretary shall affix the seal with the authority of a board, and in the presence of two directors, to all instruments required to be sealed, and shall countersign all such instruments.

143. A temporary substitute for the secretary may be appointed by the board, and the acts of the substitute so appointed shall be deemed the acts of the secretary.

SHARES.

144. 4,000 shares shall be issued as fully paid up shares to the shareholders of the Canadian Company, according to the recited articles of agreement.

145. The 4,000 shares shall be forthwith issued to the other shareholders.

146. Every share shall be indivisible.

147. Transfers of shares shall only be effected according to the statute.

148. A parent or guardian, committee, husband, executor, or administrator, respectively, of any infant, lunatic, idiot, female, or deceased shareholder, shall not as such be a shareholder.

149. Any such parent, guardian, committee, husband, executor, or administrator, may transfer any share of the infant, lunatic, idiot, female, or deceased shareholder respectively, or may become a shareholder in respect thereof, after giving to the secretary, or leaving at the office, fourteen days' notice in writing, of his desire to become such shareholder, and producing to the directors such proof of his title as reasonably satisfies the directors, and an entry shall be made in the proceedings of the directors of such proof.

150. An assignee of a bankrupt or insolvent shareholder shall not as such be a shareholder.

151. The assignees of a bankrupt or insolvent shareholder may transfer any share of the bankrupt or insolvent, after producing to the directors such proof of their title as reasonably satisfies the directors, and an entry shall be made in the proceedings of the directors of such proof.

152. A transfer of a share not fully paid up shall not be made by any person until after he has given to the secretary, or left at the office, at least seven days' notice in writing of his desire to make the transfer, and of the number of every share desired to be transferred, and of the name, residence, and description of the proposed transferee.

153. A transfer of a share fully paid up may be made to any person.

154. A transfer of a share not fully paid up shall only be made to a person expressly approved by the directors.

155. In case of the directors not approving a pro-

posed transferee of a share not fully paid up, they shall, if the proposer so require, within fourteen days after his notice of intention to transfer, either purchase the share at the market value thereof for the Company, or procure some person approved by the directors, to purchase it at such value, and take a transfer thereof, or in default of their so doing, the proposed transferee shall be deemed expressly approved by them.

156. The Company shall not be bound by, or recognize, any equitable contingent future or partial interest in any share, or any other right in respect of a share, except an absolute right thereto, in the person from time to time registered as the holder thereof, and except also as regards any parent, guardian, committee, husband, executor, administrator, or assignee of a bankrupt or insolvent, his respective right under these presents to become a shareholder in respect of or to transfer a share.

SHAREHOLDERS.

157. A person shall not be registered as the holder of a share, unless at the time of being so registered he has signed the memorandum of association of the Company, or a duplicate or a printed copy thereof, or these articles of association, or a duplicate or a printed copy thereof, or has by writing under his hand delivered to the secretary, or left at the office to be kept with the records of the Company, accepted the share.

158. A person shall not be registered as the transferee of a share until he has left the instrument of

transfer of the share, executed according to the statute, at the office, to be kept with the records of the Company, but to be produced on every reasonable request, and at the expense (if any) of the transferor, or the transferee, or his respective representatives. But in any case in which, in the judgment of the directors, this article ought not to be insisted on, they may dispense with it.

159. Every notice to a shareholder shall be sufficient if signed by the secretary, and sent by post. or otherwise, to the registered address of the shareholder; and if he be then deceased, and whether or not the Company have notice of his decease, such service of the notice shall, for all purposes of these presents, be deemed sufficient service thereof, on his heirs, executors, and administrators, and every of them.

DIVIDENDS.

160. All dividends on shares shall be declared by an ordinary meeting, and shall be made only out of the clear profits of the Company, and (but without prejudice to any preferential or guaranteed dividend) no dividend shall exceed the sum recommended to the meeting by the directors.

161. But, in order to the equalization of dividends, advances from time to time, made out of the Reserved Fund, may be applied in payment thereof.

162. The Dividends shall be yearly.

163. If and when in the judgment of the directors the accruing profits of the Company will warrant it, they may in any year order the payment of a stated amount on every share, in the nature of dividend, on account and in anticipation of the dividend for the current year.

164. In every such case the stated amount shall be so calculated as that as nearly as may be the stated amounts and the dividend shall be equal and shall be equivalent to half-yearly or quarterly dividends.

165. Every such dividend on account shall be deducted out of the then next dividend declared, and whether or not the persons entitled to the dividend declared be the persons to whom the dividend on account was paid.

166. Every dividend on account, forthwith after it is ordered, and every dividend forthwith after it is declared, shall be paid by the bankers to the shareholders on their application to the bankers for payment thereof respectively.

167. Provision shall be made by the board for payment of dividends by the bankers in Canada to shareholders resident there.

168. Provided that when any shareholder is in debt to the Company, all dividends payable to him, or a sufficient part thereof, shall be applied by the Company in or towards satisfaction of the debt.

169. The Company shall have a first and permanent lien and charge available at law and in equity, on every share of every person who is the holder, or one of several joint holders thereof, for all debts due from him,

either alone or jointly with any other person, whether a shareholder or not, to the Company at any time while he is the registered holder, or one of the registered holders of the share.

170. All dividends, on any share not having a legal and registered owner entitled to require payment thereof to him, shall remain in suspense until some person be registered as the holder of the share.

171. Unpaid dividends shall never bear interest as against the Company.

CALLS.

172. All calls in respect of shares shall be made at the discretion of the directors, but the calls on the 4,000 shares not issued as fully paid up shall be made so that those shares shall be fully called up and payable on or before Lady-day, 1860.

173. A call shall be deemed to be made at the time when the resolution authorising it was passed by a board.

174. No call shall exceed one-fourth of the value of a share, or be made within three months of a previous call.

175. The joint ho'ders of a share shall be severally as well as jointly liable to the payment of all calls in respect thereof.

176. Whenever any call is made, thirty days' notice, of the time and place of payment thereof shall be given to every shareholder liable to the payment thereof.

177. After seven days non-payment of any call in respect of any share, notice of the call shall be repeated, and, after seven days further non-payment thereof, the directors may sue the defaulting shareholder for the amount unpaid, with £10 per cent. per annum interest thereon from the day appointed for payment thereof.

178. A shareholder shall not vote, or exercise any privilege as a shareholder, while any call due from him is unpaid.

Forfeiture of Shares.

179. After forty-two days non-payment of any call, in respect of any share, the directors, with the sanction of a general meeting, may declare the share forfeited, for the benefit of the Company.

180. When any person entitled to claim a share and not having entitled himself, according to these presents, to be registered as the holder thereof, fails for six months after being thereunto required by notice from the directors so to entitle himself, the directors forthwith, after the expiration of that period, shall declare every such share forfeited for the benefit of the Company.

181. The forfeiture of a share shall involve the extinction, at the time of the forfeiture, of all interest in and all claims and demands against the Company, in respect of the share, and all other rights incident to the share, except only such of those rights as by these presents are expressly saved.

182. The forfeiture of a share shall be subject and without prejudice to all claims and demands of the Company for calls in arrear thereon, if any, and interest on the arrears, and all other claims and demands of the Company against the holder of the share when it was forfeited, and to the right of the Company to sue in respect thereof.

183. But, in the event of the Company so sueing, they shall, at such time as they think reasonable, sell the forfeited share, and set off the net proceeds thereof against the amount of their claim.

184. Forfeited shares may, at the discretion of the directors, be sold or disposed of by them, or except where a sale thereof is by these presents expressly required, be absolutely extinguished, as they deem most advantageous for the Company.

185. Provided that the forfeiture of a share may, at any time within twelve months after the forfeiture thereof is declared, be remitted by the directors at their discretion, on payment by the defaulter of all sums due from him to the Company, and all expenses occasioned by non-payment thereof, and of such a fine as the directors deem reasonable, but such remission shall not be claimable as a matter of right.

186. The forfeiture of a share shall not prejudice the right to any dividend on account, or dividend already ordered or declared thereon.

187. The sales and other dispositions of forfeited shares may be made by the directors, at such times and on such conditions as they think fit.

188. A certificate in writing, under the seal and under

the hands of two directors, and countersigned by the secretary, that a share has been duly forfeited in pursuance of these presents, and stating the time when it was forfeited, shall, in favor of every person afterwards claiming to be a holder of the share, be conclusive evidence of the facts so certified, and an entry of every such certificate shall be made in the minutes of the proceedings of the directors.

Purchase of Shares for Company.

189. Any shares may be purchased by the directors for the Company, from any persons willing to sell the same, and at such price as the directors think reasonable.

190. Provided that the directors shall not expend in the purchase of shares more in any one year than £2,000, without the sanction of a general meeting.

191. Provided that the directors shall not, without the sanction of a general meeting, apply for any such purchase any part of the revenue of the Company.

192. Shares so purchased may, at the discretion of the directors, be sold or disposed of by them, or be absolutely extinguished, as they deem most advantageous for the Company.

193. Shares so purchased shall, until sold or disposed of, or extinguished, form part of the Reserved Fund, and the dividends on account and dividends ordered and declared thereon, shall be carried to the credit of the Reserved Fund.

DISSOLUTION OF THE COMPANY.

194. The dissolution of the Company may be determined on for any purpose whatsoever, and whether the object be the absolute dissolution of the Company, or the re-construction or modification of the Company, or the amalgamation of the Company with any other Company or any other object.

195. The dissolution of the Company shall take place whenever it is determined on by special resolution, and according to the terms and conditions determined by special resolution.

196. Provided that no absolute dissolution of the Company, not being a winding up by Court under the statute, shall take place, if at or before the general meeting at which the special resolution to dissolve the Company is confirmed, any of the shareholders enter into a binding and sufficient contract to purchase on such terms as are agreed on, or failing other agreement, at par, the shares of all the shareholders who wish to retire from the Company, and make sufficient provision for their indemnity against the liabilities of the Company.

ARBITRATION.

197. Whenever any difference arises between the Company on the one hand, and any of the shareholders their heirs, executors, administrators, or assigns on the other hand, touching the true intent or construction, incidents or consequences of these presents, or of the

statute, or of any article or thing in these presents, or in the statute contained or expressed, or touching any thing to be done, executed, omitted, or suffered in pursuance of these presents, or of the statute, or otherwise, relating to the premises, or to these presents, or to the statute, or to any of the affairs of the Company, every such difference shall be referred to the arbitration of two persons.

198. One of the arbitrators shall be named by each of the parties to the difference; and, as regards any such party, whether consisting of one person or more persons than one.

199. The directors shall act on behalf of the Company in naming one of the arbitrators.

200. If either party do not, within ten days, after being thereunto requested in writing by, or by the agent of, the other party, name an arbitrator, then both arbitrators shall be named by the party by whom or by whose agent the request was made.

201. The arbitrators, before entering on the business of the reference, shall, by writing under their hands, appoint an impartial and qualified person to be their umpire.

202. If the arbitrators do not, within three days after their appointment, duly appoint an umpire, then, on the application of the arbitrators, or either of them, an umpire may be appointed by the Governor of the Bank of England; or, if he decline to make such appointment, then by the Chairman of Lloyds.

203. If the arbitrators do not, within thirty days next after the matter in difference is referred to them,

agree on their award thereon, then it shall be referred to the umpire.

204. The award of the arbitrators, or of the umpire, if made in writing, under their or his hands or hand, and ready to be delivered to the parties in difference, or such of them as desire the same, their heirs, executors, administrators, or assigns, within thirty days next after the matter in difference is referred to the arbitrators, or to the umpire, shall be binding and conclusive on all parties interested, their heirs, executors, administrators, and assigns, and all such things shall be forthwith thereafter done, omitted, and suffered as the award requires.

205. The arbitrators and the umpire respectively may, if they and he respectively think fit, make several awards instead of one award, and every such award shall be binding and conclusive as to all matters to which it extends, and as if the matter awarded on were the whole matter referred.

206. The arbitrators and the umpire respectively shall have full power to examine the books, accounts, and papers of the Company relating to the matter in difference, and to examine the parties in difference, and their respective agents and witnesses on oath, or affirmation, or on statutory declaration in lieu of oath, if required by either of the arbitrators, or by the umpire.

207. The submission to reference hereby made may at any time be made a rule of any court of law or equity on the application of any party or person interested, and the court may remit the matter to the arbitrators,

D

or to the umpire, with any directions the court think fit.

208. Full effect shall be given under the Common Law Procedure Act, 1854, and every or any other Act from time to time in force, and applicable in that behalf to the provisions of these presents touching arbitration.

Dated this 25th day of June, in the year of our Lord, 1858.

ALEXANDER MORRISON,
3, White Lion Court, Cornhill, London.

JOSEPH ROBERT MORRISON,
Theobalds, Herts.

JOHN LEACH BENNETT,
Merton, Surrey.

WILLIAM STOBART,
Cheshunt, Herts.

CHARLES TILT,
Fairlawn, Acton, Middlesex.

THOMAS LAURENCE,
3, St. Mary Axe, London.

WILLIAM MORTIMORE,
3, St. Mary Axe, London.

EDGAR P. STRINGER,
8, Austin Friars, London.

Witness to the above Signatures,

RICH^D. DAWES,
Angel Court, Throgmorton Street,
London, Solicitor.